Christmas is a Time For Giving

Written by
Linda Mereness Kleinschmidt

Illustrated by
Linda Graves

It was a few days before Christmas break and the students in Ms. Barnes' class were busy making decorations for their room. Adam, Jeremy and Rifka cut paper snowflakes. Alphonzo, LaShonda and Suzanne colored a big picture of Santa with crayons.

"What can we do for Christmas before school lets out?" asked LaShonda, putting down her crayon. "I want to <u>do</u> something."

"Me too," said Alphonzo. "Cutting snowflakes and stuff is boring."

"It beats math," said Suzanne, whose favorite subject was art and who could color for hours and hours.

Alphonzo looked out the window. "We could make a snowman or a fort or have a massive snowball fight . . ."

"In your dreams," said LaShonda. "Ms. Barnes would never let us play outside."

Jeremy stood up. "Let's plan something together. As class president, I'll be in charge. What should we do?"

LaShonda and Alphonzo rolled their eyes. Jeremy always tried to take over.

"Let's have a Christmas dance," said Rifka, smoothing her hair.

"A dance?!" All the boys looked at her in horror.

"How about going to the rink to play hockey?" said Adam, swinging an imaginary hockey stick.

Now it was the girls' turn to stare at Adam.

"No," said LaShonda. "I think the Christmas spirit means you do something for <u>other</u> people. Not for yourself."

"How about cookies?" said Alphonzo. "My sister made them last year in her class and then they passed them out to people."

Everyone glanced at each other. No one objected.

"Then let's ask Ms. Barnes!" said Jeremy.

The students did just that. In fact, they talked so fast that their teacher could hardly say a word herself.

"Okay, okay," Ms. Barnes laughed. "It sounds like you've all made up your minds. Baking Christmas cookies sounds like a great idea to me, but first we have to figure out a few details."

"Why don't we plan to bake the cookies next Tuesday morning, the last day before break," said Ms. Barnes. "I'll make sure we can use the cafeteria kitchen. But first we have to decide what kind of cookies we should bake and who we should give them to. Then, we have to bring some ingredients from home. So, what kind of cookies do you want?"

The class decided they would bake sugar cookies. Alphonzo would bring in the recipe. "We'll use all of my mom's cookie cutters," he said. "So each one will be different."

"It'll be like an art class using dough," said Suzanne, grinning. "My cookies are going to be angels."

"Mine are going to be flowers," said Rifka.

Adam frowned. "Flowers! Angels! I don't think I'm going to like this."

"Oh, hush," said LaShonda. "Just make yours look like hockey sticks."

Adam and Jeremy volunteered to bring flour, butter, sugar and the other basics for baking. Rifka, Suzanne and LaShonda said they would bring the frosting ingredients and all the dazzles to decorate the cookies.

"And who would be getting these tasty cookies?" said Ms. Barnes.

"Everyone!" the class shouted.

When next Tuesday came around, the class went to the cafeteria kitchen. With the help of Ms. Barnes, everybody measured and mixed and added the ingredients they had brought from home to make Alphonzo's recipe.

On one long table they rolled out the cookie dough, in-between grabbing bits to taste, of course. Then they pressed shaped cookie cutters into the dough and made angels, stars, snowmen, Christmas trees, candy canes, flowers and hockey sticks. Finally they placed the dough on cookie sheets and baked them to a sweet, golden brown, making the whole school smell like a bakery.

As the cookies cooled, everyone made sure they tried plenty of samples. Baking had made them hungry.

"Don't eat all our work," LaShonda reminded everyone. "Or we won't have any cookies to give away."

The students covered each cookie with thick frosting and decorated them with glitter, frosting and sprinkles—white, red, green, stripes, and swirls. Finally, they lined up rows and rows of beautiful Christmas cookies on the cookie sheets.

"Hmmm," hummed Ms. Barnes. "I think we forgot something. Did we ever decide how to wrap all of these cookies?"

The students looked at each other. Then Ms. Barnes surprised them all. She opened up a paper bag filled with plastic sandwich bags, red yarn and Christmas tags.

"What a great idea!" exclaimed Suzanne. "We can write a fancy message on each tag."

"Let's hurry," said Ms. Barnes with a smile. "We have very little time before our holiday."

Shortly before the bell rang that afternoon, the students walked through the halls, carrying baggies that held two cookies each. They gave these presents to their classmates, all the teachers, the principal, the school secretary and the custodian. Of course, they gave the most beautiful one to Ms. Barnes.

"You know," said Adam. "This is almost as much fun as hockey."

"Yeah," said Rifka. "Everyone is so happy to just get a couple of cookies."

"It's because you made them yourselves," said Ms. Barnes. "Everyone likes to get a special present like this—even me! Thank you."

Rifka, Adam and Suzanne took their cookies home on the school bus and gave one to the bus driver. When they got off, they gave cookies to the neighbors on each side of their houses.

And when Jeremy, Alphonzo, and LaShonda walked home, they gave cookies to the crossing guard on the street corner, the shopkeeper at the neighborhood grocery, and the elderly gentleman who lived alone with his dog.

On top of all that, the children saved cookies for their parents, brothers and sisters, aunts, uncles, and grandparents—and maybe one or two for themselves. With each cookie, was a tag that read:

A special treat
To make your Christmas sweet!

Jeremy	Alphonzo
Adam	LaShonda
Suzanne	Rifka

Everyone who received Christmas cookies was surprised and happy. This delighted the students because they now knew that giving was the best Christmas gift of all.

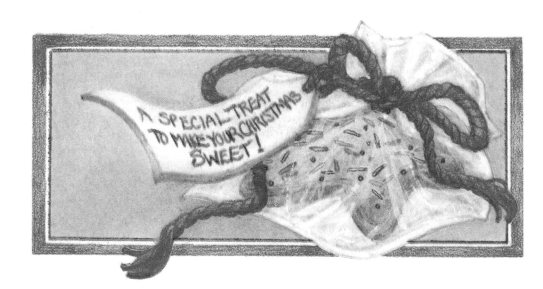